Elisapee

and Her Baby Seagull

I dedicate this book to my lovely, kind-hearted mother, Eena Kullualik, who has worked tremendously hard for us and her family, my aunts and uncles. You inspire me every day. Mom, we love you!

Published by Inhabit Media Inc.
www.inhabitmedia.com

Inhabit Media Inc. (Iqaluit) P.O. Box 11125, Iqaluit, Nunavut, X0A 1H0
(Toronto) 191 Eglinton Ave. East, Suite 301, Toronto, Ontario, M4P 1K1

Design and layout copyright © 2017 by Inhabit Media Inc.
Text copyright © 2017 by Nancy Mike
Illustrations by Charlene Chua copyright © 2017 Inhabit Media Inc.

Editors: Neil Christopher, Kelly Ward, and Kathleen Keenan
Art Director: Danny Christopher
Designer: Astrid Arijanto

We acknowledge the support of the Canada Council for the Arts for our publishing program.

This project was made possible in part by the Government of Canada.

ISBN: 978-1-77227-166-9

Library and Archives Canada Cataloguing in Publication

Mike, Nancy, author
    Elisapee : and her baby seagull / by Nancy Mike ; illustrated by Charlene Chua.

ISBN 978-1-77227-166-9 (hardcover)

    I. Chua, Charlene, 1980-, illustrator II. Title.

PS8626.I4185E45 2017   jC813'.6   C2017-906778-8

Printed in Canada.

Elisapee
and Her Baby Seagull

By Nancy Mike · Illustrated by Charlene Chua

Elisapee loved to go boating with her dad, Livee. Whenever they went out during the summertime, Livee found baby birds.

One summer, when Elisapee was seven years old, her dad brought home a baby seagull. Elisapee named her seagull "Naujaaraq," but called her "Nau" for short.

Nau was a pretty, small, grey-spotted bird. Elisapee fell in love with Nau from the moment her father brought the bird home. For the first week, Nau lived in Elisapee's house in a cardboard box.

5

Nau was always hungry. Livee taught Elisapee which foods Nau could eat. She fed Nau sculpins, seal fat, whale blubber, and even small krill. Nau, being hungry all the time, swallowed the sculpins whole with her yellow beak. Elisapee was impressed.

Nau grew, and grew, and grew! She grew white and grey feathers and had pink webbed feet.

Elisapee and her brother, Jimi, went to the shore together during low tide. At low tide, it was easy to hop from one rock to another. There, they gathered sculpins and krill for Nau to eat. They made sure to watch carefully for the tide so that they would be safe.

Once Nau got too big to live in the cardboard box, she lived on top of the family's shed. Elisapee fed her, just as her father had taught her. She even took Nau down the street to show her friends her pretty pet bird, and she and her friends chased Nau around and watched her swim in the ponds nearby.

11

Nau was loved by Elisapee. She taught Elisapee how to care, how to feed an animal, and how to have patience.

Each day, after school, Elisapee came home and rushed to find Nau. She fed Nau and hugged her, and then brought her out to play.

As the days passed, Nau grew, and grew, and grew some more!

One night, Elisapee asked her father, "How will Nau ever learn to fly?"

Livee replied, "If you throw her into the air—toward those northern lights and stars—she will fly."

Elisapee was afraid to throw her pet seagull, but knowing her father spent most days on the land and knew about many animals, she believed he was right.

15

Nau was about the size of a football and was quite heavy. Elisapee picked her up and held her for a moment. Then, gathering her strength, she threw Nau high into the air, aiming for the northern lights and the stars.

Nau fluttered her wings, but did not fly. She landed on the tundra, looking excited and scared at the same time.

On the second try, Elisapee threw
Nau even higher.

"Wooooooooow!" Elisapee
screamed, as Nau flapped her
wings and glided a little bit in
the air. But Nau soon landed
right back on the tundra.

On the third try, Elisapee was no longer scared. She was so excited for Nau to finally fly! Elisapee threw Nau once again. A gust of wind whipped against Elisapee's face, but she soon realized it was actually Nau's large wings flapping in the air. Nau was flying!

Elisapee looked up at Nau with excitement. She was finally flying! She quickly flapped her wings and climbed high into the air, gliding on the wind.

Elisapee started to feel worried that Nau might never return. But when Nau flew right above Elisapee and returned to the top of their shed, Elisapee was relieved.

After that first flight, Nau often flew around town, mixing with the other seagulls by the shoreline. Elisapee thought, *How will I know which bird is mine when there are so many other seagulls?*

Then, she had an idea . . . .

25

Elisapee found a pretty, pink, shiny ribbon in her mom's sewing box, and tied a beautiful bow on Nau's foot.

Elisapee smiled and said to Jimi, "Now we'll know where she is wherever she goes!"

Sure enough, when Elisapee saw seagulls flying along the shoreline, she knew exactly where Nau was. She watched while Nau hunted krill and sculpins on her own. Sometimes Nau even played with other seagulls.

Nau was one brave seagull. She travelled all over town and returned each night to Elisapee's shed.

One day, Elisapee came home from school and Nau was not on top of the shed.

Where could my beautiful bird be? Elisapee thought.

The next day, Nau still had not returned to the shed.

After a few more days, Elisapee knew that Nau was not coming back.

"Mom!" Elisapee cried to her mother. "Nau is gone!"

Elisapee's mom gave her a big hug and a *kunik*.🐦

"Elisapee, sometimes you have to learn to let things go," she said. "Nau will always be a beautiful spirit. She taught you many things. But she could not stay on our shed forever."

Elisapee wiped her tears and went back outside to play.

🐦 rubbing her cheek against her daughter's cheek

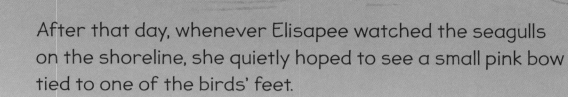

After that day, whenever Elisapee watched the seagulls on the shoreline, she quietly hoped to see a small pink bow tied to one of the birds' feet.

She often gazed into the distance of the land and the sky, watching the beautiful seagulls, and hearing them enjoy the fresh, cold Arctic air.

As she watched, she remembered Nau and her beautiful spirit.

Nancy Mike was raised in Pangnirtung, Nunavut, and continues to maintain close ties with the community. This is Nancy's first book and she is passionate about sharing stories of life growing up in Nunavut. Currently, Nancy lives in Iqaluit and works as a nurse at the hospital. She plays accordion and throat sings with the Nunavut band The Jerry Cans and travels across the world to share her stories and music. Nancy is also the mother of two beautiful girls and hopes to inspire them to love their culture and language . . . and to read as many books as they can!

Charlene Chua never had a seagull, but she once had a pigeon named Christopher that lived, for a while, in a cardboard box. The pigeon flew away, and later Charlene herself flew from Singapore to Canada (with the help of a plane, of course). She now lives in Hamilton, Ontario, with her husband and two cats, and illustrates many things, including this picture book.

Iqaluit • Toronto